RUTH DOWLEY

Top Biker

Illustrated by Strawberrie Donnelly

HODDER
Wayland

an imprint of Hodder Children's Books

Chapter One

Steve asked Kipper and me if he could
have a go on one of our bikes. But
how could he, I thought. Steve has
spina bifida. He uses sticks to help
him get around.

"Your mum will grind us into a paste
if you get hurt," I said, trying to put
him off.

"When I was little, Mum thought I wouldn't even walk, Ravi. She was over the moon when I did," said Steve.

"But don't you have trouble balancing?"

"Yeah. Because I can't feel the bottom of my feet. But on the bike, I'll be *sitting down*."

Grinning like mad, Steve put on Kipper's helmet. We looked at him geared up and ready to go. The three of us burst out laughing.

We were in the Kipps's garden. Kipper wheeled his bike to the path. I let down the saddle.

Kipper stood with one leg each side of the front wheel, holding the handlebars. "Don't roll forward!"

Steve chuckled. He leaned on me
and got on.

"OK," said Kipper. "These are the
front brakes. These are the back."

"Right." Steve gripped the handlebars.
"*Whee!*"

"*Steve!*" I said.

He grinned. "It's OK. I know I've
got to concentrate. It's just that it's
so fantastic to be on a bike."

Yeah, it *is*, I thought. After that,
I really wanted him to crack it.

Kipper and I grabbed each side of
the saddle. Steve wobbled forwards.
His feet shot off the pedals and
scuffed along the path.

"Brakes!" shouted
Kipper.

"Catch him!"
I yelled. We
closed into
a scrum.

Steve jerked to a stop.

"The saddle's the right height," he said cheerfully after we stopped laughing.

Then Steve set off again. His steering was pretty good. But, oh, those feet! They came off the pedals every few metres.

"I'm a bit *footloose!*" he joked.
"What a *drag!*" Kipper said.
"Shall we give you a *toe?*" I said.
"You pulling my *leg?*" said Steve.
We doubled up with another
giggling fit.

Steve tried sitting further back and further forward to see if it made any difference. It didn't.

"Maybe you could tie my feet on."

"That's definitely not safe!" I said.

Then Kipper snapped his fingers.

"Ravi! We should be using *your* bike."

I've got a mountain bike. The pedals
are broader and have grips.

We changed over. One of Steve's feet
stayed on all the time. The other foot
only came off twice.

"Go for it!" said Kipper the second
time down the path.

The side gate clanged. There was
a mocking hoot.

I clenched up. It was Dan Atkins.

Chapter Two

"Think he can ride a bike!" Dan
shouted. As usual, he talked *about*
Steve instead of *to* him.

I wanted to tell Dan to push off. But
I didn't want my face smashed in. He
used to be OK, but he'd become really
nasty lately.

Steve has to take a taxi to school. If Dan saw him arrive, he'd say things like, "Here's Lord Wonky-legs in his private transport." As if Steve wouldn't rather come on the bus or walk with the rest of us!

And when Miss Lowe, the nurse, fetched Steve for physio exercises, Dan would whisper, "Here comes Nanny."

I'm sure Steve heard. It must have hurt.

Dan ran up and kicked the back wheel of my bike. Steve's foot shot off the pedal and dragged.

"See?" said Dan. "If that happens even once when he's going fast, he'll come a cropper."

It was true. The hopes bouncing inside us a moment before got big punctures.

And with Dan there, the lesson was over. Steve got off my bike, looking sad.

Then Dan grabbed the bike and jumped on. He sped down the path. We all gasped. We thought he was going to crash the fence.

At the last minute, he skidded to a stop. The tyres sprayed gravel.

Dan yanked the bike around and raced back. Then he did a wheelie.

"*That's* how you ride a bike!" he yelled.

I felt like punching him for showing Steve up. How could he be so horrible? He acted like he was jealous.

Dan saw some wood and bricks stacked against Kipper's shed. He pulled out an old door. "This could be a ramp. Come on, let's make a jump."

Kipper and I weren't going to play anything that left out Steve. But we didn't know how to stop Dan. He built a jump three-quarters of the way down the path.

Steve held out the helmet. "Here."

Dan ignored him. He rode at the jump like a maniac.

The end of the ramp flipped up as he left it, but Dan kept his balance. The ramp whacked down with a bang.

"Good, huh?" he yelled.

The back door opened. Mrs Kipps came out. She saw exactly what was going on. Dan was getting a reputation with the mums and teachers.

"How about coming in for a drink, boys?" she asked.

"Great," I said. Kipper and I ran and put away the ramp and bricks.

Mrs Kipps stood and waited.

"Got to go," said Dan. He dumped the bike by Steve, sneering.

CHAPTER THREE

Steve could soon wobble down the path on his own. But that one foot kept coming off. On Saturday, we talked to his mum and dad about it.

"You've been on a bike?" gasped his mum. "It's not safe!"

"We're really careful," said Kipper. Steve's mum frowned.

Steve's dad put an arm round her. "He's still in one piece, love. The least we can do is see what happens."

Steve's mum looked worried, but came out to see. Steve rode down their drive with Kipper and me jogging each side. His mum ran along, as well.

Near the end of the drive, Steve's
foot came off. We all stopped.

"Brilliant!" shouted his dad. He
rushed up and hugged Steve. Then
he took a closer look at the pedal.
"I'm sure we can fix this to stop
you slipping."

"We must ask the doctor, too," said Steve's mum. But now she was smiling.

Kipper raised his arm. "Give us five!" Steve smacked hands with him, then with me. "To pedal power!"

Two weeks later, it was Steve's birthday. He got a bike with special pedals. His dad also put clips on the frame for his sticks if he needed to take them anywhere. We were mobile!

I gloated the first time Dan saw us out riding together. I shouldn't have.

Dan crowded close on his mountain bike, trying to make us swerve. He did it every time he saw us.

Sometimes we had to stop. Mostly
we kept riding steadily.

"Aren't you *fast?*" Dan would yell.

Chapter Four

In the holidays, Steve, Kipper and I went to the park. One day we watched some men trim a giant tree.

Branches crashed down. We sat on a bench a little way from the coned-off area.

The sun came out, and it was
really hot.

Dan cruised by. He saw Steve's bike
propped against the end of the bench.
"Having a little restie, are you?"

He rode over the grass. He started
using the cones and branches as an
obstacle course.

One of the men shouted. "Hey, you! *Scram!* Those cones mean danger."

Dan smirked as if he didn't care. He put his head down and raced out of the park.

"What a pest!" I said. "Why do his mum and dad let him get away with it?"

"His dad doesn't live with them," said Kipper. "He left last year."

"Must be rough not seeing your dad every day," said Steve.

The men went off for lunch. We were having lunch at Kipper's.

"Shall I whiz home and bring the grub out here?" Kipper asked.

"Yeah, cool!" Steve fanned himself with his jacket.

"I'll nip to the shop and get some cold drinks," I said.

Kipper gave us the thumbs up and rode off.

"See you in a minute," I said to Steve. "Don't go anywhere!"

"I'm sunbathing," said Steve.

Steve told me later that Dan came back almost as soon as I'd left. He saw that the men had gone.

Dan rode to the cones and started weaving in and out of them. He sprung and bunny-hopped a small branch. Then he got the idea of jumping a big one nearer the tree trunk.

"Watch this!" he yelled at Steve.

He got up speed and crouched over
the pedals.

The bike soared. It easily cleared
the branch. But Dan hadn't checked
where he would land. His front wheel
hit a tree root.

Chapter Five

Steve stared in horror as Dan
flew over the handle bars. He
somersaulted through the air and
crashed down on a branch with
one leg twisted behind him.

"Aaaaaah!" he screamed. "My leg!"

"Don't move!" yelled Steve.

He looked about for help. But the park seemed empty.

Steve grabbed his jacket and got off the bench. He crawled across the grass.

Dan moaned. "I'm really hurt."
Tears welled in his eyes.

"You'll be OK. Don't move," said
Steve. He gently put his jacket over
Dan. "I'll get help straight away.
Promise."

Steve crawled back to the bench and
pulled himself up. The bench steadied
him while he got on his bike.

Then he was off. Fast!

He knew there was a phone outside the park. He rode like never before.

Steve pulled up the bike close to the open phone booth and dialled 999.

Chapter Six

Dan had bruised his ribs and broken
his leg. He was in hospital for a week.
Steve wanted to visit him.

When we got to his bed, Dan looked
embarrassed. He had a cast on his leg.

"You OK?" asked Kipper.

Dan nodded.

A pair of sticks leaned on the chair
next to the bed.

"Snap!" said Steve.

Everyone laughed and relaxed.

"Oh, *don't!*" groaned Dan, clutching his chest. "It hurts!"

After a moment, he added, "Yeah. I know how it feels to have a leg that won't do what you want." He looked at Steve. "Sit down, mate."

I put Steve's and Dan's sticks together against the locker.

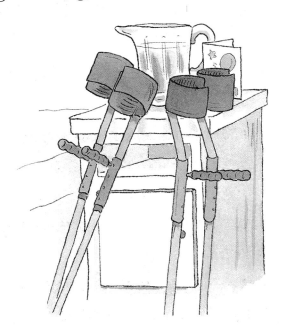

"Want to sign my plaster?" Dan asked.

While Kipper and I were signing, Dan gave Steve a poke. "Thanks for looking after me. Surprised you bothered after how I've been getting at you. I'm really sorry."

Steve grinned. "After you're better, we could all go riding together."

Wait a minute, I thought. Then I looked at Dan. He was beaming.

Kipper handed the pen to Steve.

Dan tapped the cast above his knee. "Here."

Steve signed.

"Let's have the pen," said Dan. He leaned forward. I could see it hurt his chest.

He drew an arrow to Steve's name. He wrote, "TOP BIKER!"

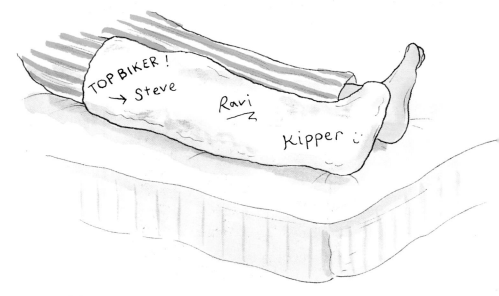

Look out for these other titles in the Shooting Stars range:

Arthur the Wizard by Peter Kavanagh
When Arthur finds his grandad's old magic staff, he wants
to learn how to be a wizard. But when he's kidnapped by
the evil duke's henchmen, Arthur finds out that being a
wizard isn't as easy as it looks.

My Dad Is... by Ali Ives
When Becky Harris has to write an essay about her dad,
she has a huge problem. She has a wonderful mum, but
she doesn't have a dad! So she decides to make one up.
But none of the dads she invents seems to be quite right.

You can buy all these books from your local bookseller,
or order them direct from the publisher. For more
information about Shooting Stars, write to: *The Sales
Department, Hodder Children's Books, a division of Hodder
Headline Limited, 338 Euston Road, London NW1 3BH.*